Fierce Competition!

By Erica David
Cover illustrated by Hollie Mengert
Interior illustrated by Francesco Legramandi
and Gabriella Matta

Random House 🏠 New York

All rights reserved. Published in the United States by Random House Children's Books,
a division of Penguin Random House LLC, 1745 Broadway, New York, NY 10019, and
in Canada by Penguin Random House Canada Limited, Toronto. Random House and
the colophon are registered trademarks of Penguin Random House LLC.

Visit us on the Web!
rhcbooks.com
dcsuperherogirls.com
dckids.com

Library of Congress Cataloging-in-Publication Data
Names: David, Erica, author. | Mengert, Hollie, illustrator.
Title: Fierce competition! / by Erica David ; illustrated by Francesco Legramandi
and Gabriella Matta.
Other titles: DC super hero girls.
Description: New York : Random House, [2020]
Identifiers: LCCN 2019020424 | ISBN 978-1-9848-9456-4 (paperback) |
ISBN 978-1-9848-9457-1 (lib. bdg.) | ISBN 978-1-9848-9458-8 (ebook)
Subjects: | BISAC: JUVENILE FICTION / Media Tie-In. | JUVENILE FICTION /
Humorous Stories.
Classification: LCC PZ7.D28197 Fie 2020 | DDC [Fic]—dc23

Printed in the United States of America
10 9 8 7 6 5 4 3 2 1

Chapter 1

The Game Is Afoot, but You May Need to Use Your Hands

Diana left the locker room ready to do her best and joined her classmates on the field. Her school would soon be hosting the Metropolis Games, a huge track-and-field meet. The events included competitions in archery, foot races, javelin throw, pole vault, and discus.

Diana couldn't wait to compete. This was where she excelled.

Of course, Diana excelled in almost every sport and class she took at her new school, Metropolis High. Her mother and the other

Amazons had prepared her well.

And it didn't hurt that she was secretly Wonder Woman, an immortal demigoddess who happened to have an extra three hundred years of training.

Still, she needed to get through the trials like everyone else. All the best athletes at Metropolis High were here. Diana got in line with the others and waited her turn.

"Next up," the track-and-field coach barked, "Minerva!"

Barbara Ann Minerva glided to the javelin runway with feline agility. Every stitch of gear she wore was perfect, from her designer headband to her expensive snow-white cleats. Her shining javelin had a tasteful hint of gold gleaming in the handle.

Then, with the most graceful run-up Diana had ever seen, Barbi set a new school record for longest throw.

Diana couldn't help herself. She exploded

into applause. "Huzzah, Barbi!" she cried. "You did it! What a run-up! What a throw!"

Barbi flipped her hair and flashed a dazzling smile. Diana's furious clapping didn't slow down until the next student, Doris Zeul, ambled up to the runway.

Doris's gear was not fancy. Her run-up exuded power but little grace. Be that as it may, when her javelin landed, no one on the field could believe it.

Doris had thrown with such accuracy that

5

she'd tied exactly with Barbi for distance— and with so much force that she'd split Barbi's fancy javelin in two.

Diana clapped and cheered again. "Well struck, Doris. Like a thunderbolt!"

Barbi shot Doris and Diana poisonous looks. But she seemed to recover quickly. "Whatever," Barbi said. "I'd already used that javelin once anyway. I'll have Father buy me a new one."

Doris simply nodded confidently and stood aside for the next competitor—Diana.

Suddenly, Diana's superior training and centuries of experience didn't feel like enough. Two records in one practice! She had her work cut out for her.

As soon as Diana started her run-up, she felt better. This event was like an old friend. Every muscle in her body knew exactly what to do. She turned along the arc and let her javelin fly. . . .

"Come on!" a gruff voice shouted behind her.

Diana turned and saw Doris and Barbi laughing.

"What was that run-up?" Barbi scoffed between giggles. "Such unusual movements. It looked like something out of ancient Greece."

"Thank you!" Diana replied, beaming. Doris let out an amused snort.

"Prince! You're first seed," the coach called from the other end of the field. Diana turned around. Barbi and Doris stopped laughing.

Diana's ancient technique had paid off; her javelin had sailed past the other two and was

still quivering in the ground where it had stuck. "Nice," their coach added when she handed the javelin back. "Zeul, second. Minerva, third. Now let's start practice."

"Top three!" Diana cheered, turning back toward the other girls. "We did it!"

Diana held up her hand to high-five as her friend Barbara Gordon had taught her to do. Doris sneered, and Barbi ignored her.

"I am speechless as well!" Diana continued gushing, not noticing the snub. "You both performed admirably. I am lucky to be here at a school with so many outstanding athletes!"

"Laps, ladies!" the coach bellowed. "Hop to it!"

Diana literally hopped to the track to start her laps. She was eager to begin training right away.

Barbi and Doris groaned and dragged their feet through the rest of practice.

Chapter 2

Down with Diana and Other Villainous Plots

After practice, Barbi Minerva scanned the field for the perfect hiding place. She needed to be ready when Diana came by so that she could ambush her.

"No one steals The Cheetah's thunder," Barbi thought. "Doesn't she know who I am?!"

Well, Barbi realized, Diana didn't actually know that Barbi was secretly The Cheetah, a super-fast, super-stealthy, super-sharp-clawed super-villain. No one could find out about that. But Diana should know that Barbara

Ann Minerva was the most popular girl at Metropolis High, and she wasn't about to be outshined by some new girl. Not without a fight. Barbi would tell her how it was going to be.

She spotted the hiding place she was looking for—it had a direct view of the door to the locker room, but she wouldn't be seen until she wanted to be. She slinked around, keeping watch for Diana.

But there was already someone here! Barbi tore her eyes away from the locker room to see Doris Zeul crouched in *her* hiding place.

"Occupied," Doris said, nudging Barbi away.

"This is *my* space," Barbi said sharply. She looked right into Doris's eyes and titled her head ever so slightly in the direction of the cafeteria.

Almost every girl at Metropolis High would have been halfway to the robotics lab by now—but Doris just shook her head.

Barbi opened her eyes a little wider and tilted her head a little more forcefully. She was used to getting her way.

Doris shook her head again and turned her attention to the locker room door.

"Doris," Barbi said finally. "Scram."

"Nope. Gotta stay here," Doris said. "Gotta be ready."

Barbi sighed. "Ready for *what*?"

"That girl," Doris said. "That javelin girl."

Barbi's eyes went wide. "You're waiting for Diana?" The new girl had beaten both their records with that one weird throw, after all.

Doris nodded. "She needs to know who's boss."

Barbi smiled. She wasn't expecting this. "My thoughts exactly," she said.

Doris looked at her. "What do you mean?"

"Have you ever noticed how easily Diana always comes out on top?" Barbi asked.

Doris grunted a begrudging yes.

"Remember homecoming? Diana stole the show with those *strange* dance moves of hers." Barbi got lost in the memory, thinking of Diana awkwardly jutting her arms and legs around. Soon everyone else had joined in with the same stiff moves.

Doris cleared her throat. "Not really my area," she said, "but still annoying."

"*Right?*" Barbi agreed. "No matter what,

she's just so . . ." Barbi's lips curled into a scowl. ". . . *nice.*"

"Everybody . . . *likes* her," Doris said sourly.

"But *I'm* supposed to be the most popular student at Metropolis High!" Barbi sputtered.

Doris narrowed her eyes. "And *I'm* supposed to be the best athlete at Metropolis High." As Doris's anger grew, it almost looked like she grew in size, too . . . just a little.

Barbi nodded. Doris might not be graceful. She might not be popular. But this once, she might be exactly what Barbi needed. She made up her mind. "A natural alliance, then. You and me." She held out her hand to Doris. Doris just looked at it.

"Think!" Barbi said. "If we work together to defeat Diana in this competition, we'll be twice as sure to succeed. Or at least make sure *she* doesn't."

"Okay," Doris said. She grabbed Barbi's hand and gave it a hard shake. "How?"

14

Barbi peeled her aching hand away from Doris's. "Well," she said, rubbing her wrist, "first things first. When Diana comes to the locker room . . ."

The locker room! They'd been so busy complaining about Diana that they'd forgotten to watch for her. Barbi and Doris craned their necks just in time to see Diana trot into the locker room. She'd walked right past them!

16

Chapter 3

Float Like a Butterfly, Sting Like a Hydraulic Power Launcher

Diana Prince was walking on air. The track-and-field practice had revved her up to train harder. She wanted to give the best showing possible at the Metropolis Games.

Luckily, Diana had more up her silver bracelets than just her Amazon skills and her superpowers. She had the best partners anyone could ask for—fellow super heroes at school. Diana had arranged for three of her best friends to meet her on the field for extra practice.

First up was pole-vaulting. While she waited for her partner, Diana did some warm-up runs.

Pole-vaulting was complicated. She made her approach, planted her pole, and swung up, twisting over and around the bar. On each run she cleared it by a little bit more.

Just as Diana landed softly in the bag after her fourth practice run, she heard a familiar voice say, "Not bad, but I'll show you how it's done!"

Then her friend Kara Danvers hurtled over the bar, clearing it by a huge distance and . . .

. . . falling straight toward her! *YIKES!*

Diana scrambled to get out of the way. But after a moment had passed, she still hadn't heard Kara hit the bag. She looked up to see her friend hovering just above her.

"Ha!" Kara laughed as Diana tumbled off the bag and got ready for the next run. "I bet you've never seen a vault like *that,* have you?"

"Never!" Diana agreed, laughing. "But in the future, will you please utilize the pole? It helps with the illusion."

Unlike most people, Diana had the privilege of knowing the super hero identities of her closest friends. Kara was also known as Supergirl, an alien from another planet who had superhuman abilities here on Earth—including the power of flight.

Kara zipped up to the bar and positioned it a little higher. Diana examined it from the ground. She wasn't sure she'd ever cleared one that high.

"We'll go at the same time," Kara suggested, grabbing a pole. "Don't worry if we start to crash; I'll fly out of the way."

Diana nodded and prepared her approach. Then both girls took off. Diana could feel Kara running a nose ahead of her. She knew that Kara's super-speed would allow her to fly around the world in the time it took Diana to do one vault. Her friend was controlling her speed to help motivate her. She pushed a little harder.

"Let's do this!" Kara shouted as they approached the box.

They planted their poles at the same moment and went sailing toward the bar. Kara flew at the exact height she needed to just clear it. Diana's feet cleared the bar, but her shoulder

caught it during the twist. The bar tumbled down with the girls.

"Yes!" Diana cheered.

"Yes?" Kara asked.

"I did not make it this time," Diana explained. "But I could tell from that run that I *will* be able to do it."

"You got that right!" Kara said, pumping her fist. "Let's go again."

The girls got back into position to start their next run. Diana planted her feet firmly. "By the winged sandals of Hermes, I will take to the skies one day, too, Kara Danvers!"

Next up was archery practice. When Karen Beecher saw Diana across the field, she waved and accidentally dropped the satchel she'd been carrying. Diana heard Karen's concerned *Eep!* and saw her friend hastily gather up her belongings and scurry in her direction.

"I'm here, Diana!" Karen said when she made it to the archery field. "Why'd you want me to bring my extra stinger launcher?" She opened her satchel and revealed two gizmos she had made.

Diana picked one up, aiming it at the archery target. It made a loud buzzing sound as a tiny arrow flew out toward the target. But just before it hit the bull's-eye, it twisted into a weird curlicue and came flying back toward the girls.

"Great Hera!" Diana said, and took off running.

"Wait!" Karen cried. "Oh no." She hurried after her friend.

Diana snuck a peek behind her as she ran. The little arrow followed her no matter how much she zigged and zagged.

"Drop the launcher!" Karen called out. Diana obeyed and kept running. *Bzzzzt!* Diana stopped when she saw that the arrow had

zipped right back into place on the launcher. Her mouth fell open and she turned to her friend.

"I'm sorry!" Karen squeaked, finally catching up with Diana. "I've been experimenting with a self-retracting stinger that comes back to the launcher after it's deployed. No need for manual reloading. But it's not quite there yet."

Karen Beecher didn't have super-speed like Supergirl or the powers of a demigoddess like

Wonder Woman, but she was super smart . . . and super nerdy. She spent most of her time coming up with high-tech gadgets in her workshop. She had already built herself a whole super-suit that let her become the hero Bumblebee. But sometimes her inventions were a bit glitchy.

"I didn't know you were going to shoot it so far!" Karen explained. "Here, take my main stinger launcher. It's much more stable. The new one is still in the testing stages." She switched out the launchers.

Diana tried a few shots with the other launcher. She aimed well but got no bull's-eyes.

"Maybe try it with the adjustable scope a few times," Karen suggested, snapping an attachment into place. "Once you're more comfortable, you can try again without it."

This was exactly the kind of practice Diana was hoping for. "I may not float like a

butterfly—or like Supergirl," she told Karen as she took aim again, "but maybe I can learn to sting like a bee."

The final friend Diana expected today was Barbara Gordon. She'd enlisted Barbara's help with the javelin throw. The trial had gone well, but she'd seen firsthand how tough the competition would be. She wanted more intense training.

"I did not expect it to be *this* intense," Diana said as Babs dragged a gigantic catapult across the field.

"You wanted a strong competitor for javelin practice," Babs said. She hopped onto the contraption and made a few adjustments while Diana took it in.

It looked like a medieval catapult. But instead of a bucket for holding a boulder, it had a long shaft that held a javelin spear. It also held countless replacement spears waiting for automatic reloading.

"I saw something like it in a book," Babs explained. "Or maybe it was a movie. Or a video game. Not sure. But I tell ya, it sure makes me want to try to beat it. And I don't even throw javelin."

Babs slid off the catapult, doing a tidy little somersault into a standing position, and pulled a remote control from her Utility Belt. Babs was also known as Batgirl—her lifelong admiration for Batman had led her to teach herself acrobatics, stealth, and of course, the hottest tech—and apparently this was her latest invention.

"Ready?" Babs asked. "Let's see how many *you* can throw in one minute."

"In javelin, it is not about how many you can throw—" Diana began.

"Go!" Babs shouted, and slammed her hand against the start button. "Go, go, go!"

The catapult lurched into action. It hissed and steamed. Then it started flinging javelins across the field faster than seemed possible. Regardless of the logic of it, Diana's competitive spirit kicked in. She tossed javelins while Babs handed her replacement after replacement.

One long minute later, Diana collapsed onto the field, panting. The catapult was no worse for wear. But . . .

"Yes! YES!" Babs cheered. "A perfect tie! You almost beat my machine!" She gave Diana a hand and pulled her to her feet.

Diana went back to the runway and tried a traditional run-up and throw. She was tired, but her arm was stronger and her throwing motion felt more natural. The exercise had helped after all.

Diana smiled and high-fived Babs. With her friends on her team, she couldn't lose.

Chapter 4

It's All Fun and Games Until the Ferris Wheel Breaks Down

Day after day, Diana trained for the Metropolis Games with her super hero friends. But one afternoon, just as she was expecting Kara, Diana heard buzzing. At first she thought Karen was early for her portion of training, but then she saw that her cell phone was making the noise. It *was* Karen, though not in person.

"I can't make it to practice today," Karen said timidly when Diana picked up. "All five of my older brothers are getting awards today—in different places. I'll be buzzing around Metropolis all day trying to make each ceremony."

"By Hephaestus's beard, that is wonderful!" Diana said. Karen's brothers were all heroes in their own right—though not super heroes.

"I know," Karen said in a quiet voice. "I still hate to miss out."

"You need not worry," Diana reassured her. "Until tomorrow, Karen Beecher."

As soon as she'd hung up, a text came in from Babs. It took Diana a minute to open it— she was still getting used to the trappings of the World of Man—but she finally got it.

> Can't make practice. Got called in. This is the big one!

Diana furiously typed back.

> Dearest Barbara,
> Batman needs your assistance??? Are you all right?

> **Do you need backup?**
> **Yours sincerely,**
> **Diana Prince**

The reply came faster than Diana thought anyone would be able to type.

> **No. They need me for a double shift at BURRITO BUCKET. This is it!!!!!!! See you tomorrow.**
> **XOXO**

Babs absolutely loved her after-school job at the Burrito Bucket. Diana knew it was a big honor for her to be asked to do two shifts in a row. She typed back her congratulations as Kara arrived.

"I can't stay," Kara said as Diana tucked away her phone. "You-know-who called, and Krypton forbid anyone not drop everything for him."

"Your cousin?" Diana asked. Kara's cousin Clark had the exact same powers that Kara

did. But he had arrived on Earth first, so he got all the recognition and glory. And to make matters worse, since he was considered the more important hero, he was always trying to boss Kara around.

"We're having a family dinner. I have to fly to Smallville," Kara said with a supersized eye roll. "I could do without another evening with Clark, but I don't want to disappoint the Kents. I'll be back for pole-vaulting tomorrow."

Diana waved goodbye as Kara flew away. "Only you and me today," she said out loud to her track-and-field equipment. She spent the rest of the afternoon alternating sprints with discus throws.

As she was walking home from her solo practice, Diana noticed that a carnival had set up in the Metropolis fairgrounds. Then she

noticed something strange about the Ferris wheel. It looked like someone was stuck in one of the cars.

Diana quickly ducked behind a hedge and changed into her Wonder Woman gear. She sprinted toward the Ferris wheel to see what was going on.

"Wonder Woman!" the ride operator cried when he saw her. "The Ferris wheel broke down. I can't get it moving. And . . . and . . ." He gestured toward the top of the wheel. A small child was at the very top.

"Hi, Wonder Woman!" the child called out. She waved to the hero.

"Hold on, small child! I will reach you with the speed of swift-footed Hermes," Wonder Woman shouted. The hero nimbly bounded up the spokes of the towering Ferris wheel.

The crowd gasped in alarm.

Soon she had reached the little girl. "Let us go for a ride together, shall we?" she said. She unfurled her Golden Lasso and tied it to one of the beams of the wheel. The little girl put her arms 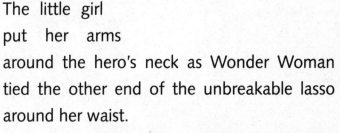 around the hero's neck as Wonder Woman tied the other end of the unbreakable lasso around her waist.

"This is AWESOME!" the little girl squealed as Wonder Woman rappelled them down to the ground.

"Hooray, Wonder Woman!" the crowd cheered. Barbi Minerva turned away from the Skee-Ball lane just in time to see Wonder Woman deftly swing the last few feet down to the ground, holding some kid in one arm.

"Wow," she heard Doris Zeul say from the lane next to her.

"That Wonder Woman is such an attention hog," Barbi scoffed. "Where was my applause when I got four high scores in a row?" Barbi and Doris had been practicing their hand-eye coordination by playing Doris's favorite carnival game.

"Still," Doris admitted. "Cool moves."

"I suppose Wonder Woman is an impressive athlete," Barbi said, envy creeping into her voice. "At least we don't have to compete against *her* in the Metropolis Games. Diana Prince has nothing on Wonder Woman . . . or on us."

Barbi and Doris crept into the crowd. The

little girl's mother was thanking Wonder Woman over and over.

"We're so lucky to have you," the woman gushed. "You're such an excellent role model for our children. I hope little Penelope grows up to be just like you."

"Yeah! I wanna be like Wonder Woman!" Penelope started to climb up the Ferris wheel again, trying to reenact her own rescue. "Penelope to the rescue!"

"Wait!" Wonder Woman pulled Penelope down and set her back on the ground. She crouched to the girl's level and looked her right in the eye. "You do not have to be just like me," Wonder Woman told her. "You only have to be just like you. Looking up to your heroes is wonderful—I had a great mentor to help me achieve my dreams. But the *most* important thing is to be kind to others. That can do more good than any superpower."

Barbi rolled her eyes at this, but Penelope's

mother ate it up. "Can we get a picture?" she blurted out.

As Wonder Woman posed for selfies with Penelope and her mother, Barbi thought over what she'd just heard. "Kindness . . . ," she muttered.

"Yeah, kindness," Doris scoffed. "So annoying. Like that javelin girl."

"I bet if Diana met Wonder Woman, she would fall for that kindness nonsense even more than Ms. For-the-Children over here," Barbi said.

"Psh," Doris said. "She'd fall for anything."

"That's it!" Barbi exclaimed, feeling a moment of evil inspiration. "We'll beat Diana at her own game! Shower her with kindness, pretend to be her friends . . . That Goody Two-shoes will eat it up with a spoon! Then"—Barbi punched one fist into her other hand with a loud *smack*—"we sabotage her the day of the games."

Barbi shot Doris one of her sweetest smiles. "What do you think?"

"Yeah," Doris said, squeezing the ball she was holding until the leather binding cracked at the seams.

The two girls wandered back into the carnival, plotting and planning the whole way.

Chapter 5

Messenger Pigeons, Eye Problems, and Very Distant Cousins

The next morning, Diana Prince woke up feeling happy. The Ferris wheel rescue had gone well, and everyone had been so nice to her afterward. It felt good to make a difference. If she hadn't decided to come to the World of Man, she never would have had these experiences.

"Coo!"

"Yes, it is cool," Diana said, rubbing the sleep out of her eyes. "Wait, what?"

"Coo! Coo!" *Flapflapflap!* "Coo!"

The sound was coming from outside the window. Diana got out of bed and opened the blinds. She saw a big gray pigeon flapping against the side of the building.

"Oh!" She quickly opened the window, and the pigeon flew into her room. It landed on her physics homework and looked at her with an annoyed—but dignified—expression.

"Welcome!" Diana said. It looked like a Themysciran homing pigeon to her. Her people used them to send messages hundreds of miles. Then she noticed a scroll of paper wrapped around its leg. She gently pulled it off.

Its job done, the pigeon flapped out the window and out of sight. Diana unfurled the scroll and read the message. It was from her mother.

Dearest Diana,

Greetings from your one and only home of Themyscira. I and your fellow Amazon warriors think of you often, though we are also busy with our training, which goes excellently as usual.

I remain perplexed at your insistence to leave our home for the World of Man and your subterfuge in achieving this goal. However, I admit your decisive victory in the Tournament of Athena and Aphrodite and the Twenty-One Challenges was impressive, as befits my daughter. Surely by now your superior skills have solved all the problems in the World of Man. Why have you not returned? Has your training lapsed?

I am understandably concerned that you are unable to rise to this challenge. I shall dispatch a guardian to keep watch and ensure your success.

Yours sincerely,

Your Mother,

Hippolyta, Queen of the Amazons

"Oh no," Diana said. Her mother was clearly still angry that Diana had entered the Twenty-One Challenges in disguise. It had been the only way to come to the World of Man!

But this? A guardian sent by Hippolyta would be nothing but trouble. She hoped whoever she was sending wouldn't arrive until after the Metropolis Games.

That afternoon, Diana threw herself into her training. She had to prove to her mother that she was as disciplined as ever and ready to tackle the problems of the World of Man. She wanted to stay.

She and Kara squared up for another attempt at the pole vault. Diana was clearing the highest bars she ever had, thanks to Kara's coaching and her own determination. They

ran the length of the runway, planted their poles, and—

"What?" Diana screeched to a stop. Right in front of her, between her and the bar, stood a giant with one great big eye and a blank expression on its face. "Uhh . . ."

"Hey!" Kara barked. She leaped into action, changing into Supergirl at super-speed. She assumed the intruder was a monster of some kind. "Move it or *lose it*!"

Diana didn't move a muscle. Neither did the cyclops.

Kara followed through with her threat. She hit the stonelike giant with all the power granted to her by Earth's yellow sun. The cyclops didn't flinch. It didn't fight back. It didn't even budge.

"Excuse me!" Kara said. "It's kind of rude to just *stand* here blocking the pole vault and not even fight back!"

43

"Desist in your efforts, Kara Danvers. We are in no danger," Diana said, finally coming to her senses. "I think I know why this cyclops is here." She looked up into the giant's one big eye. It stared right back at her. "And I think we are going to need some help."

Diana asked Kara to bring Karen, Babs, Jessica, and Zee to meet her at the picnic tables behind

the school. If she could trust anyone with this secret, it was her five best friends. When they arrived, the cyclops was no longer at the pole vault. It was right behind Diana.

"My friends," Diana said. "This is a guardian sent by my mother, Hippolyta, Queen of the Amazons."

All five girls blinked at her for a moment. They looked up at the cyclops, then back at Diana. Then they blinked again.

Babs waved her hand in front of its one eye a few times. The cyclops was motionless and unresponsive, yet all the girls got the distinct impression that it was watching them.

"A Themysciran guardian does not speak. It does not interfere. It watches. In this case, this one is watching me. Everything this giant sees, my mother also sees."

"Surely we can . . . make it disappear somehow?" Zee Zatara said. She was not only an assistant in her father's magic show, she

45

was also an honest-to-goodness sorceress. She called herself Zatanna. She was supernaturally good at magic . . . most of the time. But Diana knew it was no match for her mother's magic this time. She shook her head.

"It is magically tied to me and will be until my mother calls it home."

"Can it even move?" Jessica Cruz asked. She activated her Green Lantern power ring and flew up to take a better look at the giant's face.

Diana stood up and walked to another table to demonstrate. The giant awkwardly put one foot in front of the other until it was the same distance away from Diana that it had been before.

"I hate to be the one to say it, Diana," Babs piped up, "but I think someone might notice this guy following you around all the time."

"And there's the one eye thing," Karen said quietly.

46

"That is why I need your help," Diana explained.

"Perhaps we can . . . *transform* it into something a little less noticeable," Zee said. She conjured a makeup crayon and got to work on the giant's face. When she pulled away, the other girls all jumped in surprise.

"Two eyes! Like a human!" Zee said. "No good?"

Zee had drawn a second eye on the cyclops. But because its real eye was in the center of its face, she'd had to squeeze the other eye off to the side. It made the giant look even stranger than before.

Babs pulled her cowl out of her backpack and arranged it over the giant's face.

"Now it just looks like a giant with a purple mask," Kara said.

"How about these?" Karen pulled out a pair of wraparound sunglasses. They hid the eye pretty well. Zee fetched a wig and a scarf from the drama club's costume closet, and Diana topped it off with a baseball cap.

The girls stood back and looked at their work. The cyclops was still almost seven feet tall, but looked more like a human than before. It would have to do.

"So . . . ," Karen said. "We'll just say he's your cousin . . . from Greece?"

"Polyphemus," Diana confirmed.

"Poly-*wha*?" Kara said. "I'm just gonna call him Phil."

"Cousin Phil," Babs said.

The girls walked back to the pole vault, with Phil ambling stiffly along behind them.

Chapter 6

Playing Nice—
It's Harder Than You Think

Kara Danvers wasn't sure Cousin Phil's disguise would work, but they didn't have a choice. Apparently only Diana's mother had the power to take him away. And with the Metropolis Games right around the corner, Diana couldn't stop training. And she also couldn't miss class.

Kara was walking with Diana—with Phil following a few feet behind—and helping her explain him to the other students.

"Hark!" Oliver Queen called out as he

leaped into view. "*Who* is this strapping fellow?" Oliver always talked like he was in an old movie just to be dramatic.

Diana introduced Oliver to her cousin Phil. Phil didn't react, but Oliver didn't seem to notice.

"Tall fellow, isn't he?" Oliver observed.

"He, uh . . . he plays basketball," Kara improvised.

Oliver looked closely at Phil for a moment. The girls held their breath. Then he nodded,

seeming satisfied. "If you are anything like Diana, then we are in for an excellent season!"

Oliver slapped Phil on the back and continued on his merry way.

"Well, that was easier than I thought it would be," Kara muttered to Diana.

"Excuse me!" Lois Lane hurried in their direction. "I'm on deadline, and I have to get some students on record for my story."

"I'll comment," Kara said, trying to casually position herself between Lois and Phil.

"On my story about the condition of the boys' locker room?" Lois scoffed, and tried to reach around Kara. "The principal says the cleaning schedule has already been doubled, everything is sparkling, and if the boys want it tidier, they can get to scrubbing. Any comment?" She held her voice recorder as close to Phil's face as she could reach.

Behind his sunglasses, Phil seemed non-committal.

Lois fell back, disappointed. "Not much of a talker, is he?" she said to Kara.

"He's the strong, silent type," Kara replied quickly. "Literally," she added under her breath. Lois was about to try again when she saw another group of boys and chased them down the hall, recorder in hand.

"Good thing *she* didn't notice anything strange about Phil," Kara said. "It would have ended up all over the school paper."

Kara turned to watch Phil as they continued outside to the practice field. His wig wobbled back and forth as he awkwardly lurched behind them.

When they got to the field, Doris Zeul was waiting for them. Kara got ready with another Phil excuse, but Doris didn't even seem to notice him.

"Greetings . . . Diana . . . darrr-ling?" Doris said in a halting voice. She seemed to be having a difficult time forming the pleasant words with her mouth. Kara made a face like she was hearing nails on a chalkboard.

"Doris!" Diana said with a smile. "Are you practicing today as well?"

"Your . . . technique . . . is . . . fabulous?" Doris continued, ignoring Diana's question. "I . . . am . . . not . . . worthy?"

"Do not be silly!" Diana protested. "Your trial run was inspiring!"

"Doris, are you okay?" Kara asked. Doris was never nice. She never rated anyone else's athletics above her own. In fact, Doris normally never talked to them at all. She ran with a rougher crowd.

"I . . . need . . . your . . . help?" Doris said. "Will . . . you . . . be . . . my . . ." She stopped talking. It seemed like she was waiting for something. "My . . ." Then she grabbed

her right ear and wiggled it. "My . . ."

". . . your track-and-field mentor?" Diana offered. "Doris, what an honor! Especially from an athlete of your ability!"

Doris turned and looked in the direction of the girls' locker room. Then she looked back at Diana. "Hold on a sec," she said, and hurried away.

Doris felt herself getting angry. She didn't want to lose control. But she had to find out what was going on. She found Barbi in the girls' locker room. Doris pulled the earpiece out of her ear and threw it at her partner in crime.

"What was that?" she barked.

"Why did you ask her to be your mentor?" Barbi asked. "You were supposed to say 'practice buddy'!"

"I couldn't hear you!" Doris said. Barbi had forced Doris to wear an earpiece so that she

could tell her what to say to Diana. Doris wasn't used to talking to people much—especially in a nice way. But this had turned out worse than she would have done on her own.

Now she wouldn't just have to hang around with that goody-goody. She wouldn't just have to be nice. Now she had to pretend to learn from her.

This wasn't going to be easy. Doris had a secret: She had used a growth serum to make her as powerful as the strongest animals on Earth. She could even become as large as she wanted as the formidable Giganta. But when her strength and size came out, so did her animal instincts. They were sometimes hard to control.

"It doesn't matter anyway," Barbi said, interrupting Doris's thoughts. "Just train with Diana and be nice."

For Doris, those two things didn't go together. At all.

"Something is off with Doris," Kara said to Diana as they set up for pole vault practice. "She didn't even notice Phil."

"Perhaps she was being polite," Diana said, eyeing the guardian.

"Doris? Polite? And she would never ask someone else to mentor her," Kara pointed out. "She thinks she's the greatest athlete *ever*!"

"Maybe she has turned over a new leaf!" Diana said. "If so, we should encourage her."

"Maybe . . . ," Kara said. "Just be careful with her."

Doris returned from the locker room and joined them at the pole vault. She spoke more like her usual self, but she had a strange smile plastered on her face.

"Okay, let's do this . . . mentor." Doris had a pained look as she muttered that last word.

But Diana didn't seem to notice. The three girls got to work practicing pole vault.

"Kara, can you pass me a pole . . . please?" Doris asked. Diana gave Kara a meaningful look and went to line up for the first run. Maybe Doris really was trying to learn to be nice. But as soon as Diana wasn't looking, Doris swiped the pole out of Kara's hand with a sneer. Then she shoved her out of the way so that she could stand next to Diana in Kara's usual place.

"Now, Doris Zeul," Diana said, "in my experience, pole vault is all about believing in yourself."

"Great tip, coach," Doris said, gritting her teeth.

"I know it seems almost impossible to get over that bar," Diana went on.

"Maybe for you," Kara heard Doris mutter. Diana didn't hear.

"But if you think positive, you can do anything!" With that, Diana started her run-up. Phil slowly followed.

To Kara, it looked like Doris was practically vibrating with anger. In fact, Kara could swear that Doris looked like she was growing. And when Doris took her turn at the pole vault, she looked stronger than Kara had ever seen her.

Chapter 7

Moving Targets, Catapult Catastrophes, and Other Natural Disasters

Karen Beecher had noticed a sharp improvement in Diana's aim since they'd started practicing archery together. Diana had always been one of the best archers, thanks to her Amazon training. But Karen's stinger launcher had stepped up her game.

Luckily, Cousin Phil usually stayed *behind* Diana. Karen didn't want to know what would happen if one of her stingers bounced off him.

Kara had told Karen all about Doris's strange behavior at pole vault practice. Diana was sure that Doris's intentions were pure, but her friends agreed that something fishy was going on. So when Barbara Ann Minerva glided toward the archery area during practice, Karen wasn't surprised.

"Diana, darling," Barbi cooed, "you haven't introduced me to your dashing visitor yet."

"This is my guardi—that is, cousin. From Greece," Diana said. Karen could tell it was hard for Diana to lie.

"Phil," Karen added.

"Hello, handsome." Barbi held out her hand to Cousin Phil. He didn't take it. He didn't move at all. "He's charming," Barbi said anyway. "I adore his ensemble."

Karen raised an eyebrow. An actual compliment from Barbi Minerva? About clothing? The closest thing to a compliment Karen had ever heard from her was the time

Barbi had said that Karen's leg warmers really distracted from how absolutely gaudy her striped sweater was.

Plus, there was no way Barbi liked Phil's outfit. It looked terrible.

"Say, Diana," Barbi went on, "I was thinking that we top three need to stick together. What do you say we help each other practice?"

"I'm helping her practice," Karen piped up.

"And we would love to have you join us," Diana said. "The more the merrier!"

Diana took her first shot with Karen's launcher, getting very close to the bull's-eye.

"Stunning opener, teammate!" Barbi cheered. "Did you see that, Phil, my friend?"

Diana smiled, and to Karen's great surprise, Diana and Barbi high-fived. Was it possible?

63

Was Barbi actually being supportive of her classmate?

Karen shrugged and got in place to take her turn at the target. She was all lined up for the perfect bull's-eye. She got no kickback from the launcher. But just as the stinger was about to strike—*fwoop!*—the target slid to the side. The stinger flew right past it.

"Bad luck, darling," Barbi said. Karen turned to look at her. "We can't all be good

at . . . *something*." Her snide remark was the first time Karen had seen the real Barbi all afternoon. She looked to see if Diana had noticed, but she was busy adjusting her scope.

Karen was going to be keeping an eye on Barbara Ann Minerva.

Later that day, Babs was making adjustments to her javelin catapult when she spotted a trio of girls—and one giant lumbering cyclops— walking toward her. It was Diana . . . with Barbi Minerva and Doris Zeul. So the other girls were right. These two really had won their friend over.

"I told Barbi and Doris all about your catapult, Babs!" Diana gushed. "They want to try to beat it!"

"I bet they do," Babs said.

"It's quite an accomplishment, Barbara," Barbi said. "Don't you agree, Doris?"

"Sure," Doris said. She smiled, and Babs winced. It was a hard smile to look at.

Babs popped her gum and looked at Diana. She seemed thrilled to have two new practice partners. Babs shrugged and set up the catapult for another showdown.

"Ready, set . . . go!" Babs flipped the switch on the machine and hurried over to Barbi to hand her javelins. Diana did the same for Doris.

All three competitors—Barbi, Doris, and the catapult—started flinging javelins. But after only a few throws, Babs's contraption suddenly turned ninety degrees and started shooting javelins straight down into the ground! By the time a minute was up, there was a bouquet of broken javelins sticking out of a deep hole in the grass.

"Gordon!" the track-and-field coach called from the long jump area. "You're cleaning that up!"

Babs slumped over and examined her

machine. There were a few pieces missing
from the place where the arm attached to the
frame. They couldn't have fallen out on their
own, she knew. Someone had taken them out
on purpose.

While Diana ran to pick up the rest of the
javelins, Barbi and Doris circled Babs.

"What a shame," Barbi said sarcastically.

"Yeah," Doris said. "Too bad."

"Great practice, pal!" Barbi congratulated Diana. "See you tomorrow!" When Diana looked up and waved, Barbi and Doris were all smiles. Then they sauntered away.

"Gee, Cousin Phil," Babs said when they were gone. "I wonder who sabotaged my catapult. Did you see?"

Phil only stared back.

Chapter 8

Dodo's Revenge . . . You Won't Like Her When She's Hangry

A few days later, Doris Zeul sighed with relief at the sound of the lunch bell. She had been training with her new mentor every afternoon. The extra energy she had to put into being nice *and* staying calm meant her appetite had gone through the roof. She couldn't wait to sit in gloomy silence and eat her lunch.

But as Doris turned the corner into the cafeteria, she saw the last two faces she wanted to see—Diana Prince and her weird cousin Phil. *Ugh.*

"My favorite mentee!" Diana cheered. "I invite you to sit with my friends this lunch period."

"But . . ." Doris made eye contact with Barbi Minerva, who was sitting at a table with Carol Ferris and Leslie Willis. Barbi rolled her finger as if to say, "Keep things rolling." Doris was getting used to reading these clues from her new ally. She had to eat with Diana. *Ugh.*

"Next to me!" Diana said. Doris sat down and looked around at the other girls uncomfortably. Kara Danvers, Barbara Gordon, Zee Zatara, Jessica Cruz, and Karen Beecher were all staring back at her. They didn't trust her, she could tell. The feeling was mutual.

But Diana couldn't know that. Doris tried to smile.

"I believe we should take our mentorship to the next level," Diana was saying. "We could do some good by volunteering at the animal

shelter together. Or perhaps assist in cleaning up the park."

More work? Doris was already spending all her free time trying to beat Diana Prince at her own game. How much of her life was she going to have to spend pretending to be nice? "I don't know . . ."

"And even better, we can both don *these*!" Diana held up two pairs of socks as though they were trophies. They were the same—blue with white stars. She handed one pair to Doris, who stared at them, stunned.

"We will be quite a *pair*! Do you not think so, Dodo?"

Doris looked up from the socks. "What did you call me?" she growled. Doris knew she didn't talk fancy, but she was no dodo. She felt her muscles start to grow. She tried to control her anger. Being nice was sickening. And she hadn't even had a bite of her lunch yet.

"Dodo!" Diana repeated. "Where I come from we do not have nicknames, but Babs has taught me all about them. She said one usually makes the name shorter, and sometimes it is said twice. Therefore, *Dodo*!"

Doris looked at Babs, who was staring back in stunned silence. Then she looked back at Diana, who smiled at her with the most sincere face she had ever seen. *Ugh.* This was it. She couldn't take it anymore.

Doris stood up. As naturally as she could, she made her way out of the cafeteria. She didn't want to give up on the plan, but

she just couldn't be nice anymore. She was wired from so much training. She was angry about that awful nickname. And she was so, so *hungry*.

Doris slipped out of sight. She looked around to make sure no one could see her. *Finally!!!* She couldn't hold it in anymore. She grew into Giganta. The plan was forgotten—it was time to eat!

After school, Diana wasn't sure where her new friends Doris and Barbi had gone. She walked home with her usual crew—Kara, Babs, Zee, Jessica, and Karen—and of course, Cousin Phil wasn't far behind.

The other girls were trying to convince Diana that Barbi and Doris were up to no good, but Diana wasn't so sure.

"They sabotaged my catapult!" Babs sputtered.

"That could have been anybody!" Diana said.

"What about that moving archery target?" Karen asked.

Diana sighed. "I know Barbi and Doris are not my usual compatriots," she said, "but neither were any of you when I first arrived. My mother would have had me avoid everyone but Amazons. She was wrong about you. I believe everyone has the potential for good."

Kara was about to respond to this, but just as they turned the corner toward the Metro-Narrows Bridge, sirens started to blare.

The six friends wasted no time. They changed into their super hero gear and raced toward the trouble. Cousin Phil followed at his usual slow pace.

When the bridge came into view, Diana saw the problem. A ten-foot-tall woman with wild red hair was stomping around—Giganta. She towered over the cars, occasionally leaning

74

over to swipe one out of her way. Frightened people abandoned their vehicles and ran.

It looked like Giganta was trying to get to Vito's Veggie Dog food truck. It was shaped like a hot dog. And to the giant villain, it looked *delicious*!

Wonder Woman and her friends sprang into action.

Supergirl got there first. "*Frank*ly," she said, "I think she's just hungry." Supergirl tried to lift the truck out of Giganta's reach. But Giganta's arms were so long that she was still able to swat it. The truck tumbled out of Supergirl's grasp.

Luckily, Green Lantern was waiting below with her power ring. She used it to form a huge hot dog bun out of energy. It caught the food truck easily and softened its landing.

"Giganta's working her *buns* off trying to get to that veggie dog!" she said.

Wonder Woman managed to get her lasso around one of Giganta's ankles. Batgirl got her grappling hook around the other. Giganta stumbled, accidentally kicking the Veggie Dog truck. "No!" she cried, reaching out for it while it spun away.

Zatanna conjured a pile of condiments to slow the truck's spin. It squished to a stop. "I *relish* the chance to save that dog!" she joked.

Bumblebee buzzed around, trying to distract Giganta. Just when Wonder Woman was sure Giganta was about to swat Bumblebee into outer space, she saw her friend zip behind Cousin Phil. Giganta stopped in her tracks.

To everyone's surprise, Giganta wouldn't take her eyes off Cousin Phil. She stopped swatting at cars and instead combed her hands

through her hair. She . . . smiled? (Again, it was hard to look at.)

While Giganta was distracted, Supergirl flew to the Veggie Dog truck. She landed on the roof and thumped it twice. "Hit it, Vito!"

Vito put the food truck into gear and hit the gas. His wheels spun for a moment, spraying condiments everywhere. Then he was off.

By the time Giganta came to her senses, Vito and his Veggie Dog truck were out of sight. Giganta seemed disappointed, but she didn't do any more damage. She dashed off into the evening. The super hero girls stayed on the scene to make sure everyone was safe.

"Wow," Zatanna said, using her magic to make the globs of ketchup and mustard disappear. "Cousin Phil really came through for us this time."

"Any chance he'll stick around?" Green Lantern asked Wonder Woman.

"That is for my mother to decide," Wonder Woman said.

"One thing's for sure," Batgirl said. "He was the *weiner* of that fight."

"What a fun way to pronounce the word 'winner,'" Wonder Woman thought.

Chapter 9

Real Babs, Fake Babs, and the Call of the Wild

The afternoon after their battle with Giganta, the girls decided they deserved a treat.

"Let's go to Sweet Justice," Jessica said to Diana. "I want to buy Cousin Phil a smoothie!"

"Thank you, Jessica Cruz," Diana replied, "but I must continue to train with Babs for the Metropolis Games. Her commitment to our success has put us on the path to glory— Apollo's strength be with us!"

"Me?" Babs asked, confused. "I didn't know we were training today."

"Yoo-hoo! Di! Di, darling!" a voice called

from across the street. It was Barbi Minerva.

"Babs!" Diana trotted over to Barbi and pulled her into the group.

"Babs? *I'm* Babs," Babs said, a little hurt.

Diana turned to Babs. "As I said, we are using nicknames in our training group. Barbara Ann Minerva has the same first name as you, Barbara Gordon. So you must have the same nickname! Babs!"

Babs tried to catch Barbi's eye. Surely she wasn't okay with sharing a nickname; Barbi always wanted to stand out. But Barbi simply smiled.

"Thank you for teaching me about nicknames, Babs!" Diana said. "Let us go, Babs!"

Diana, Barbi, and Cousin Phil made their way toward the practice field, leaving the rest of the girls scratching their heads—and the real Babs pouting.

To Barbi's surprise, when they got to the field, Diana didn't stop. She kept on walking straight into the woods behind Metropolis High. Her weird cousin followed silently, as usual.

Now what? As if this nickname business wasn't confusing enough.

"Oh, Di?" Barbi called out. "Where are we going?"

"It is a surprise, Babs!" Diana replied. "We are almost there!"

They hiked through the woods silently, until a strange apparatus came into view above them.

Diana turned to Barbi for the big reveal. "Surprise!" she said. "To freshen our training regimen and strengthen our bond as teammates, I have constructed a ropes course!"

Barbi looked up at the jumble of ropes, nets, logs, and platforms in front of her. It was nothing she couldn't handle, of course— when she was The Cheetah. She had the climbing skills of a jungle cat. But these ropes were grimy, the wood was splintered, and the ground . . .

Barbi sighed. The ground below it was absolutely *covered* in mud. She looked down

at her spotless white designer sneakers. "Goodbye, beauties," she thought.

"We will work through the course together," Diana explained. "A group effort!"

"I could do this course with one paw tied behind my back without any help from the likes of you," Barbi thought. But to Diana she only smiled sweetly and said, "Sounds heavenly."

It was not heavenly. The first thing Barbi had to do was give Diana a boost over the climbing wall. Dirt from the bottom of Diana's sneakers sprinkled all over her perfect outfit. Barbi turned and looked at Cousin Phil, who was silently watching.

"You could help, you know," she said to the giant.

"What did you say?" Diana asked, accidentally stepping right on Barbi's head. She got to the top of the wall and looked back down, holding out a hand to help Barbi up.

Barbi gritted her teeth into a smile, shook

85

some dirt from her hair, and took Diana's hand. "Nothing. You're doing amazing, sweetie."

Diana beamed and helped her up. Next they had to climb the net. Right below was the muddiest patch of the course. Barbi sharpened her focus. A little dirt was one thing. Falling into *that* was not an option.

Or so she thought. Diana's climbing technique was as strange as her javelin run-up. She managed to jostle the net so much that Barbi had a hard time holding on. Just when she thought she'd secured her grip— *"Yow!"*—Diana stepped on her hand. Barbi went tumbling off, landing softly in the mud.

"My deepest apologies!" Diana called out immediately.

Barbi looked up, covered in mud, and saw Diana's face. She was absolutely 100 percent sincere. It had been an accident. Barbi had to keep pretending to be nice. She let out an awkward laugh and tried to compose herself.

"You can do it, Babs!" Diana cheered her on as Barbi climbed back up the net. "*We* can do it, together!"

The next obstacle was the Tarzan swings. First Barbi watched as Diana flung herself from rope to rope, making it to the other side. Even under the layer of mud, Barbi smiled. Diana was a good athlete, but *this* was what Barbi knew how to do best.

Barbi grabbed the first rope, pulled back, and took off. Flying through the air felt great. It had been forever since she'd stalked the forest

as The Cheetah. She'd almost forgotten how much she hated training with Diana, when—

Snap!

Barbi's rope broke. She tried to grab for another, but it was covered in a green moss that made it hard to grip from this angle. She slipped and fell, landing in a huge pile of rotting dead leaves.

"Babs!" Diana cried. "Babs, are you all right?"

Barbi stood up slowly. Because of the mud already covering her, the dead leaves stuck to her body, her hair, and even her face. There were probably even bugs and worms in this pile. Barbi shuddered.

"Babs!" Diana kept saying. "Babs!"

Barbi let the rage take over. The more she

88

heard that stupid nickname, the more Diana sounded like prey, not teammate. Barbi was done with training. "I am not Babs," she snarled. She ducked into the darkness of the woods.

"I am The Cheetah," she growled, transforming as soon as she was out of sight.

Diana didn't know where Barbi had gone. She thought she saw a pile of leaves shift below the Tarzan swings, but then she saw nothing. If they were going to finish this ropes course, they had to do it together. Teamwork was the whole point.

Then Diana heard a low growl. She suddenly had a strange feeling deep in her gut. It felt like being . . . hunted.

She scanned the tree line for signs of a predator. Just as her gaze settled on two shining yellow eyes, it leaped!

Diana didn't have time to get a good look. She took off, scaling the remaining obstacles. There was some kind of jungle animal chasing her!

She climbed a ladder, scrambled up a slanted log, and sprinted across a tightrope. Whatever was behind her had no trouble with any of the tests of agility. It was getting closer and closer.

If only this creature was one of her practice partners and not trying to attack her!

Finally Diana reached the final obstacle—a zip line. She grabbed the only trolley and took off, gliding down the wire toward the end platform. She landed, doubled over and panting.

All was quiet. Diana looked up at the top platform and thought she saw a furry creature slink off into the darkness.

A few moments later, Diana heard rustling in the nearby trees. She braced herself for another attack. But it was only Cousin Phil.

Before she could breathe a sigh of relief, the bushes rustled again.

Barbi emerged, covered in mud and leaves.

"You will not believe it, Babs!" Diana said, relieved to see her friend. "I think I saw a fierce mountain lion! Are you all right? Did you see it?"

"Mountain lion? In these woods?" Barbi said. She didn't look surprised. "Not likely. But let's get out of here, just in case."

At Sweet Justice, the rest of Diana's friends were drinking their celebratory smoothies. The topic of conversation was Barbi and Doris.

"Why are they being so nice to Diana?" Jessica asked.

"And so mean to us!" Karen added.

"Well, that's not unusual," Zee said.

"There's no way Barbi would let someone

call her Babs," Babs pointed out, still stewing about the stolen nickname.

"And *no one* would let anyone call them Dodo," Kara said.

The girls all laughed.

Suddenly someone zipped to the side of the table. "What's so funny?" Barry Allen asked. "I like jokes!" Barry was one of their classmates. He worked the counter at Sweet Justice.

"Oh, ah . . . we were just discussing the Metropolis Games," Kara explained, clearing her throat.

Squish, squish, squish. Barry's friend Garth caught up to him. "That's no joke," he said.

"Diana has some serious work ahead of her."

"What do you mean?" Babs asked.

"Doris and Barbi," Garth said. All five girls perked up at the mention of those two names. "They will stop at nothing to win. And I mean *nothing*."

"Do you think . . . ," Jessica offered, "that they might even try . . . being nice?"

Barry laughed. "Oh, now I see the joke," he said. "That would be a stretch for them. But I

wouldn't be surprised if they tried something a little more *evil*."

He cleared the table and went back to the counter. Garth followed him.

"Evil like cheating?" Karen whispered to the other girls.

"Or sabotaging someone's equipment?" Babs added.

"We'll never convince Diana that Barbi and Doris have bad intentions," Kara said. "We're going to have to have her back *for* her."

Chapter 10

Cheaters Never Win . . . but Sometimes Cheetahs Do

Finally, the day of the Metropolis Games arrived. Barbi didn't think she would make it much longer pretending to be nice to Diana. She'd lost her temper so badly at the ropes course that she'd almost given everything away! Luckily, Diana didn't suspect that the animal hunting her had been Barbi herself.

But now she was so close. Her plans were about to fall into place.

Doris ambled up and gave Barbi a discreet nod. Barbi winked back and watched the spectacle on the field. The bleachers were full of people from all over Metropolis. Competitors from the best schools in the city warmed up on the field.

Barbi saw Diana Prince arrive with her gaggle of good girls. They were all cheering her on and wishing her good luck—without any ulterior motive! It was so strange.

"Babs! Dodo!" Diana called. Barbi could feel Doris vibrating with annoyance next to her.

"Keep it cool, Dodo," Barbi muttered. "Just a little longer."

Doris's eyes stabbed her with daggers as she grumbled unhappily.

Diana trotted to the archery field with Cousin Phil and Karen Beecher following. Karen was carrying Diana's archery gear. Barbi had no idea why the cousin was there. To be supportive, she guessed. She rolled her eyes.

Barbi steeled herself for a few more hours of being nice. "Di! You're here!" She slunk

97

around Diana and hip-checked Karen behind her back. She caught Diana's bow when Karen almost dropped it. "Careful, Karen," Barbi said. "Don't worry; I can take it from here."

She slid over to Doris while Karen said good luck to Diana, and together they made the swap. Barbi smiled and handed Diana the replacement bow just in time. The only one who saw the switch was Diana's cousin, and Barbi knew he wasn't going to say anything.

Barbi batted her eyes at Phil while she

strode to her mark. She would be first up in the archery event. She gave the crowd a winning smile, nocked her arrow, pulled back, and—

Thwap! A perfect bull's-eye.

"Still got it," Barbi said as she struck a pose and waved to the cheering people. Diana was clapping so hard that her applause almost drowned out the rest of the crowd's.

Doris was next. Barbi could tell she wanted to pull her famous move again—tying Barbi's bull's-eye by splitting her arrow. But Doris looked angry. And they could both hear Diana saying, "Go, Dodo! Go, Dodo!" over and over. Doris wouldn't be able to pull off that move without being perfectly calm.

Still, her arrow came very close.

"Absolutely beautiful shot," Barbi said over

the sound of Diana's frantic cheering.

"Don't pull that fake nice stuff on me," Doris grumbled.

"It's not fake, Dodo, my dear," Barbi said. "Any shot that doesn't beat mine is a beautiful shot."

Doris frowned and turned to watch Diana.

Diana was thrilled that her little team was off to such a good start. Watching Barbi and Doris succeed had her jazzed up to take her own turn.

She went to her mark. She nocked her arrow. She pulled back, and—

Thud. Her arrow went straight into the ground.

What? How was that even possible?

Diana only had two more tries at hitting the target. She squared up again, pulled back, and—

Snap! This time her bowstring broke! She turned and looked at her teammates. Barbi looked back, wide-eyed, and Doris shrugged. Phil didn't react. Diana asked the referee if she could switch bows, and he nodded.

With the new bow in hand, Diana finally got off a straight shot. It flew at the target, and—

Fwoop! The target moved out of the way! The arrow flew right past it! Diana blinked. She must have imagined *that.*

"What a shame, Di," Barbi purred in her ear as the other archers took their turns. "It's just bad luck. Your form was lovely."

When the archery event was over, Diana was in last place. But at least her friends Barbi and Doris were first and second.

Karen Beecher was watching the event from the stands. She knew Diana didn't imagine that target moving. It was the same trick someone had played on her during practice. And it just so happened that Barbara Ann Minerva had been there for both mishaps.

"Did you see that, girls?" Karen asked. Babs, Jessica, Zee, and Kara all nodded.

Kara and Babs stood up. It was time to investigate.

Chapter 11

The Not-So-Sweet Smell of Sabotage

Babs and Kara snuck into the girls' locker room, hoping to find clues. They wanted proof that Barbi and Doris were sabotaging Diana—and to find out how. Babs took out her forensic kit and carefully dusted the equipment cage for fingerprints.

Kara stalked through the rows of lockers, flinging open each door. "AHA!" she shouted. "AHA!"

"What are you doing?" Babs whispered.

"I want to be ready in case we catch them red-handed," Kara explained.

"They're not in the lockers, they're out on the field," Babs said.

"But look!" Kara said. Babs joined her by the lockers. She took a closer look and saw deep scratches in some of the doors.

"These almost look like . . . ," Babs said.

"Claw marks," Kara said, confirming her suspicions. Babs looked up at the label on the locker with the most scratches; it was Diana's.

"If it turns out these games are being sabotaged by werewolves, I'm going to be very confused," Kara said.

Babs and Kara slipped back out of the locker room and ran straight into Cousin Phil.

"AHA!" Kara said, pointing at Phil. "Huh?" Kara craned her neck around Phil and looked toward the field. Diana was there, helping the coach pile discuses. The guardian had never been this far from Diana since it had arrived. And it never had its back to her. It always just followed and watched Diana. Now, instead, it was staring right at Kara and Babs.

"Could he be . . . following *us* now?" Babs asked, trying to get a closer look at Phil's face.

Phil, as always, revealed nothing. Kara and Babs shrugged and returned to the bleachers.

"How's our girl doing?" Babs asked when they got there.

"She crashed into the bar during pole vault," Zee said. Kara knew this was next to impossible. She hadn't seen Diana hit a bar since their first day of practice.

"Then her javelin went *way* off course," Karen said. "The way it was moving . . . it reminded me of the remote-controlled drone you and I built together, Babs."

Babs furrowed her brow.

"Luckily she blew them all away in the foot race," Jessica said. "She's in fifth place overall, thanks to that event alone."

"Who's on top?" Babs asked.

"Guess," the other girls all said in unison.

Barbara Ann Minerva was feeling great. She was in first place, her ally Doris was in second, and Diana Prince was so far behind there was hardly any point in continuing to sabotage her. That faulty pole and remote-control javelin had done the trick perfectly. And the best part was that they were able to just hand the sabotaged equipment right to Diana. She trusted them.

Barbi smiled and preened while the final event was being set up.

"Hey," Doris said, nudging Barbi.

"Careful, dear," Barbi said, adjusting her jersey. "This cost more than . . . well, than anything you have."

"*You* better be careful," Doris grunted. "*Dear.*"

Barbi looked at her ally with surprise. "What

are you so grumpy about? Our plan is working. You were worried about Diana outshining you. She's not. Problem solved. You should be thanking me."

"*I* should be beating *you*," Doris said.

Barbi scoffed. "That wasn't part of our agreement."

"No," Doris argued. "You're the popular one. I'm the strong one. That's the agreement."

"Stronger than The Cheetah?" Barbi

thought, and laughed. Who did this girl think she was? She let out a low, feral growl.

Doris's anger was radiating off her. When she gritted her teeth and balled her fists, it almost looked like her shoulders were getting bigger. . . .

Chapter 12

The Old Switcheroo and the New Cousin Phil

Karen Beecher decided to get a closer look at the final event—the discus throw. If it was anything like the other events, there was a good chance someone was going to mess with Diana's equipment.

And Karen had a hunch it would be Barbi or Doris doing the messing.

Karen transformed into Bumblebee and buzzed over to the pile of discuses. No one would notice her. She was too small. From there, she could watch the preparations for the event.

After the discuses were handed out, Bumblebee *did* see Barbi and Doris messing with the equipment.

"Just as we suspected," Bumblebee said. "But . . . but what the double cross?"

It wasn't Diana's discus they'd switched out—it was each other's!

She watched as first Barbi casually slinked over to the bleachers and pulled a discus out from under them. Then she glided over  to Doris's warm-up area and swapped the new discus for hers. Doris didn't notice. Her attention was laser-focused on the scoreboard.

Bumblebee wondered if Doris could put herself in first place by sheer will.

With her trick pulled off, Barbi leaned over to lace up her brand-new pair of perfectly white cleats. That was when Bumblebee saw Doris tear her eyes away from the scoreboard and examine her discus. She looked up, vibrating with anger and staring right at Barbi. Then she switched the new discus for Barbi's. She was back in her place by the time Barbi stood up from lacing her cleats.

It seemed the villains had turned on each other after all. Still, Bumblebee didn't think it was fair that one of them should be stuck with the trick discus. They should *both* have an equal chance to win . . . or lose. She formed a plan, transformed back into Karen, and grabbed the trick discus.

Then she ran smack into something big and hard. She looked up and saw Cousin Phil. He had somehow appeared in her path!

Karen jumped back. Why was Cousin Phil here? Why was he blocking her way? Did he

112

disapprove of her spying? Did he think she should not get involved? *Was she going to get in trouble?*

But then Karen saw Phil do something she'd never seen him do before. He winked his one giant eye. It was so fast, she wasn't sure that she had really seen it. Then he slowly stepped aside.

Karen had the feeling Phil did *not* disapprove of her plan. She got to work.

Diana waited for the final event to begin. She did not have much chance of coming out on top, but she could still do her mother proud in the discus throw. "At least Babs and Dodo are doing well," she thought.

She watched as Doris ambled to the circle. She got into position, took a few turns back and forth, then started spinning.

The only problem was, Doris didn't stop spinning. She didn't release her discus. She just kept spinning and spinning.

It wasn't until the ref shouted, "Disqualified!" that Doris finally stopped. She threw the discus to the ground and stomped over to Barbi.

Somehow she looked

twice the size she had when she'd started her attempt.

"What was that?" Doris shouted in Barbi's face. "I couldn't let go!"

"I don't know!" Barbi said. "It was supposed to go backward!"

"What?" Doris thundered. "You mean *Prince's* was supposed to go backward!"

Diana gasped. Her friends had been right! Barbi and Doris were trying to sabotage her equipment! But then why had Doris's throw gone wrong?

While Barbi and Doris argued, Diana thought she saw Bumblebee buzzing around the discus circle. But she couldn't be sure.

"Minerva!" the coach shouted. "Less talking, more chucking! You're up!"

Barbi tried to compose herself as Doris stared her down. She picked up her discus and gave it a close look. She didn't appear to find anything wrong with it. She carried it to

the circle and prepared her stance. Then she made a graceful turn and a half and released the discus.

It flew . . . but not forward. Not backward, either. It simply kept spinning, rising higher and higher into the air directly above the circle. Then it suddenly fell. Barbi barely moved out of the way in time to avoid being clobbered by it.

Barbi growled and turned toward Doris. Diana had never seen Barbi so angry. She almost looked like a predator about to pounce. It reminded her of something. . . .

"Zero yards!" the ref called out. Diana looked up at the scoreboard. Barbi's and Doris's failures left room for *anyone* to come in first in the Metropolis Games.

1 BARBARA ANN MINERVA
2 DORIS ZEUL
3 DIANA PRINCE
4 WEIN-PERE
5 MARST

Chapter 13

Sometimes Socks Just Aren't Enough

Diana didn't know where to focus. Barbi and Doris were squabbling. The competitors from other schools were jumping on their chance to take first place with their own discus throws. Then Bumblebee buzzed up to Diana and transformed into Karen when no one was looking. Babs, Kara, Jessica, and Zee all joined them on the field.

"I saw Barbi and Doris *both* switch out the equipment," Karen said. "So I might have given them a little taste of their own medicine. Because I'm pretty sure they did the same to your pole, javelin, bow, and target."

Diana had to admit it made sense. She was so disappointed. "Perhaps fake Babs was not the brightest star in Zeus's heaven," she said to her friends, "but I am deeply disappointed in Dodo." Diana thought they had forged a connection worthy of Amazon sisterhood. They even had matching socks!

"It's all right, Diana," Kara said. "Now it's all cleared up. There's nothing stopping you from smashing that discus throw and coming out on top!"

"Thanks to you," Diana said, looking at her *real* sisters in arms—Kara, Babs, Karen, Jessica, and Zee. "I was so wrapped up in being Dodo's mentor, I ignored my mentors. My best friends. Thank you for helping me train and for defending me from my saboteurs."

As Diana gazed at her friends in admiration, they all caught an unexpected movement in the corner of their eyes. All six heads turned in

unison to see Cousin Phil extend his stiff arm. He handed an object to Diana. It was a deep blue with golden stars all over it.

"Apollo's bright light! My old discus from back home!" Diana exclaimed in surprise. "But where did—"

"Prince!" the coach called. "You're up!"

Diana nodded to Phil and the rest of her friends. With them behind her, she felt like she had already won. She walked to the circle and took her stance.

Barbi was near the end of her rope with Doris. "I was in first place!" she snapped. "Now some bozo from Metro Academy will probably win! *Weeks* of planning down the drain! All for your ego, Doris!"

"*My* ego?" Doris growled. "MY ego?"

"Wait!" Barbi saw Diana Prince walk up to the discus circle. She was the last one to take a turn at the last event in the tournament. She

would have to beat the top score by a huge margin . . . but it wasn't impossible.

Diana took a long look at her weird cousin Phil, still standing there and staring after all this time. He was surrounded by Diana's other friends . . . her real friends.

Barbi and Doris both held their breath. Then Diana wound up, spun around in that ancient way of hers, and—

The bleachers erupted in cheers. Diana had absolutely demolished the record. The scoreboard updated with the new data.

Diana Prince had won first place in the Metropolis Games.

Barbi and Doris both flew into a rage. Not only had they failed to win, they hadn't even beaten Diana—the one person they had gone to all this trouble to beat!

They thundered up to the ref. "Excuse me, *kind* sir, but I'm afraid there's been some sort of mistake," Barbi said, trying to stay as calm as possible. She was starting to feel as angry as she had that day on the ropes course. "Ms. *Prince* or one of her little cohorts sabotaged my discus."

The ref looked back at her, confused. "Aren't you one of her cohorts?"

"Doesn't matter!" Doris grunted. "SHE CHEATED!"

Barbi nodded so vigorously that—*plop!*—the remote control fell out of her pocket.

The ref looked at the fallen device. "What

123

was that you said about cheating?"

Karen picked up the remote and examined it. "I bet you used this to guide Diana's javelin out of bounds!" she said.

Barbi didn't know what to say. Except . . . "It was Doris!" She pointed one perfectly manicured finger at her former ally. "She was the mastermind!"

"What?" Doris fumed. "No!"

"And who came up with all this?" a voice said. Barbi looked up and saw the rest of Diana's friends—each holding the sabotaged javelin, bow, pole, and target.

The ref and the judges disqualified Barbi and Doris on the spot.

Chapter 14

Cheetahs and Hippos and Monkeys, Oh My!

Diana watched, amazed and disappointed, as her two former practice partners stomped away from the field in opposite directions in clouds of rage.

"They were only pretending to be nice to me," Diana said. "I guess they were only pretending to be nice to each other as well."

Before she could give it another thought, Diana was swept up by a crowd of friends and fellow athletes and led to the podium for the medal ceremony.

But just as one of the judges was about to

place the gold medal around Diana's neck, a cacophony of beeps rose up from every corner of the field and bleachers. The crowd looked at their phones and started running in different directions.

Babs leaped to the top of the podium, phone in hand. "It's Giganta and The Cheetah," she whispered. Diana didn't wait to get her medal. She hurried under the bleachers with her friends so they could change into their super hero gear and make a plan.

"According to the emergency alert we all got, Giganta is terrorizing the mall," Batgirl explained. "The Cheetah is wreaking havoc at the zoo."

"I can take The Cheetah on my own," Wonder Woman said. She turned and looked at Cousin Phil. "Well, *kind of* on my own. It will take all five of you to handle Giganta. We will join you when we can."

The girls agreed and split up. Batgirl, Green

Lantern, Supergirl, Bumblebee, and Zatanna all went to the mall. Wonder Woman headed to the zoo. Cousin Phil lumbered behind her.

"I wish we were here for sightseeing, Cousin," she said as she examined the huge claw marks across the METROPOLIS ZOO sign. She followed the trail of mayhem and spilled popcorn to the sea lion enclosure. The Cheetah was crouched on the pile of rocks in the center, holding a bucket of fish and throwing them at the horrified tourists. The sea lions didn't look too happy about it, either.

Splat! A fish landed right in someone's ice cream. Wonder Woman grimaced at the sight of it and shouted, "Cheetah!"

The Cheetah let out a low growl and arched her back like a jungle cat. Even from here Wonder Woman could see how big and sharp her claws were. And she was angry. She looked right into Wonder Woman's eyes and crept closer. Wonder Woman felt a familiar

tingle down her spine—the same feeling she had when the creature was hunting her at the ropes course.

The Cheetah pounced! Wonder Woman braced herself for the attack, and the two tumbled across the pavement toward the monkey enclosure. Towering above them were nets, ropes, and platforms high on poles for the monkeys to play on.

The Cheetah leaped up the ropes and lashed out with her claws at Wonder Woman from above. The monkeys screeched—and stayed out of The Cheetah's way.

Wonder Woman didn't know why The Cheetah was doing this. But she knew she needed her to leave these people and animals alone. She nimbly climbed the monkey ropes. The Cheetah followed her across the enclosure, swinging from platform to platform.

The ropes course in the woods had been good practice for this battle. But The Cheetah

was so fast. Soon the villain was swinging back and forth over the hippo enclosure.

Then, to Wonder Woman's surprise, The Cheetah reached behind her and pulled out a discus! *Her* discus! The blue and gold one that Cousin Phil had given her. How had The Cheetah gotten hold of it?

The Cheetah let out a savage growl. Then she landed on the nearest platform; spun a graceful, powerful spin; and let go of the discus. It flew toward Wonder Woman with amazing speed. She didn't have time to dodge it, so she braced herself. Then—

Doink! Cousin Phil had moved in front of her! He blocked the discus, and it went spinning back toward The Cheetah.

The Cheetah grabbed the discus as it hit her in the gut and sent her flying back toward the hippo enclosure—

Splash!

Barbara Ann Minerva sputtered and splashed as she came to the surface. She'd changed back from The Cheetah when she hit the cold water. Cats hate getting wet, after all.

She looked up and saw Wonder Woman on the monkey ropes searching for her. Barbi realized she must have lost control after being disqualified. The zoo usually calmed her down because she felt at home here. But even so, that Goody Two-shoes Wonder Woman was the last person she would have wanted to see.

Barbi ducked behind a big rock and watched until Wonder Woman and that tall guy with her were out of sight.

"*Hmm* . . . he looks familiar," Barbi said to

herself. But before she could think about it, the rock she was hiding behind began to move. It turned and looked at her with two big round eyes.

It opened its enormous mouth and sent a wall of disgusting hot air into her face. It wasn't a rock. It was a hippo, probably thinking she was about to give him a snack. That was when Barbi realized she was swimming in a pool full of hippos.

"*Ew* . . . hippo saliva and slimy algae," Barbi said, cringing.

She hurried out of the pool and went home to lick her wounds.

Meanwhile, across town, Batgirl and the other super heroes tore through the hallways of the Metropolis Mall, looking for Giganta. As Batgirl cartwheeled over a kiosk selling personalized cat sweatshirts, the girl at the register called

out, "Food court!" Batgirl waved her thanks and pivoted toward the smell of greasy eats. Her friends were right by her side.

The first thing she saw when they got there was the Mexican food stand, Taco Swell. Giganta wasn't there, but the place looked like it had exploded—there was salsa, guacamole, and tiny little strips of lettuce everywhere.

"Are you guys okay?" Batgirl asked the people working there. Batgirl was absolutely loyal to her job at Burrito Bucket, of course. But she didn't wish this even on their biggest competitor.

The Taco Swell employee hiding behind the counter nodded and pointed in the direction of Harry's Hoagies. Batgirl and her friends all turned to see Giganta practically dangling from the sign above the sandwich shop. The sign was shaped like a giant sandwich— and it looked like Giganta was trying to get it down.

"What is it with this lady and giant food?" Bumblebee said.

"If you were a ten-foot lady on a rampage, I bet you'd get pretty hungry, too," Supergirl said.

"I mean, I guess?" Bumblebee said, and they both took off flying. They tried to pry the sign out of Giganta's grip. But as soon as they had one hand free, Giganta would grab it with the other one.

The five friends formed a circle around Giganta and tried to contain her damage.

"Giganta!" Batgirl called out. "Hands off the hoagie! Let's talk!"

Giganta simply looked at them, reached up, and ripped the sign from the rafters. Nuts and bolts sprinkled down from the ceiling. Without

taking her eyes off the heroes surrounding her, she put the giant hoagie in her mouth and bit down—

"*Ahhhh!*" Giganta seemed to grow two more feet when the pain and frustration hit her. It wasn't a real sandwich, of course. She couldn't eat it. Batgirl and her friends braced for battle as Giganta held the giant hoagie like a baseball bat, reared back, and—

Smiled?

Batgirl turned and saw that Wonder Woman had arrived. But that wasn't what had stopped Giganta in her tracks. It was . . .

. . . Cousin Phil.

Wonder Woman had arrived at the mall ready to jump in and join her friends in their battle. But the moment Giganta saw Cousin Phil, she

stopped rampaging and started grinning the strangest grin Wonder Woman had ever seen. A grin even stranger than the one Doris had on her face when pretending to be nice.

While Giganta mugged at Cousin Phil, Green Lantern wasted no time. She used her power ring to form an energy cage around Giganta. That would contain her until the authorities arrived. Giganta hardly noticed. She just kept on staring at Cousin Phil, clearly smitten.

Supergirl looked at Giganta, then back at

Cousin Phil. His face was blank, as usual, but she could swear he was blushing.

"What . . . just . . . happened?" Supergirl asked.

"Maybe it's better not to know?" Bumblebee suggested in a quiet voice.

"Agreed," Green Lantern and Zatanna said in unison. Then all the heroes high-fived.

Epilogue

So Long, Cousin Phil!
It Was Great Seeing You
with Your One Eye and All

The next day, things had calmed down. Babs, Kara, Zee, Jessica, and Karen were sitting at their usual table at Sweet Justice. They were pretty sure that this time, Diana would show up for their post-battle brain freeze. There were no more Metropolis Games to train for, after all.

But when Diana did arrive, there was something . . . *different* about her.

"What is it?" Zee asked, circling Diana. "A new outfit?"

"A new ring?" asked Jessica.

"A new flowery perfume?" Karen suggested, sniffing the air.

"Are you carrying more books than usual?" Kara asked.

Babs didn't even look up from her phone. "It's Cousin Phil."

"Oh!" Jessica said. "Cousin Phil! Where is he?"

Diana whipped her head around and looked for him. He wasn't in his usual place ten feet behind her. He wasn't anywhere nearby. "I suppose my mother, Queen Hippolyta, called him back," she said. "Perhaps I proved I do not need a guardian after all."

"Or," Babs said, "she saw you don't need one. Because you have us."

"Yes!" Karen said, winking. "We can keep an eye on you just as well as he can."

"You can keep many eyes on me, Karen Beecher!" Diana said. "Phil only had one,

and you each have two!" She sat down and plunged her straw into the frosty smoothie in front of her. She raised her glass and said, "By the many eyes of Argus!"

"By the many eyes of Argus," they all replied, clinking their glasses together.